The Oracle

by Joe Queenan and T.J Elliott

https://offthewallplays.com

The Oracle written by Joe Queenan & T.J. Elliott was originally produced by Knowledge Workings Theater (Marjorie Phillips Elliott, Executive Producer) at THEATER FOR THE NEW CITY in May 2022 with direction by T.J. Elliott, lighting design by Mikelle Kelly, set design by Kathleen Ritter, and sound and visual effects by Luke Lutz. Emma Denson served as an associate producer. The production stage manager was Morgan Lindsey Fears assisted by Aislinn Cain. The cast was as follows:

BART .... Hassan Hope

MICKY .... Jasmine Dorothy Haefner

AISLING .... Alyssa Poon

LEO .... Patrick Smith

FRED .... Ed Altman

Characters

CAST (In order of appearance)

- **Bart Little**, an African American man in his late 20s, who is the very new, very eager assistant to Micky Cohen

- **Micky Cohen**, a White woman in her early 30s, who juggles her demanding job as Head of Information Services reporting to Leo Sweeney and partnering with her same-sex spouse in the parenting of their two children

- **Aisling OToole**, a young Asian American woman, a Harvard post-grad bearing all the attitude that usually entails, and the CEO's new hire as a second Oracle

- **Leo Sweeney**, an older, vibrant White man, who is the corporation's so-called "Oracle"—officially titled the Chief Knowledge Officer, an engaging know-it-all

- **Fred Spee**, another White man who is the longtime CEO of the corporation, top dog with equal parts bark, bite, and blandishment

Scene **1**

Early morning at a multibillion-dollar corporation in the 21st century

LIGHTS rise to show us a raised platform at center stage rear with a screen above it and angled steps on either side leading up to it. The screen reads: 'Do It Yesterday.'

Upstage left, there is an overhang at an angle tilting up, creating a kind of alcove, which represents a space off the boiler room. Beneath the overhang are some boxes indicating its cellar position, and along the backstage wall in this nook is a large dartboard. Far stage right is an office break room with an oval table surrounded by a few modern chairs.

BART LITTLE stands at the table, taking sheets of paper out of a bin and sorting them into piles. MICKY COHEN enters stage right, her arms filled with folders sporting large numbers from 1 to 12.

MICKY

You're here already, Bart?

BART

Hey, Micky. Figured best to be early on the first day of a new assignment. Came in with my dad. Is Leo already here?

MICKY

Before eight AM?

Places folders down, shaking her head

Ill-advised. At these ritualistic human sacrifices, Leo discourages being the early bird.

Sorts the papers that BART handled into folders

BART

He compares his presentations to human sacrifice?

MICKY

Don't worry. The rituals are bloodless. Leo jokes that the only real excitement at our (*makes air quotes*) three reveals comes from this crowd's stampede for the free bagels.

BART

Laughing

Yes, I've heard that one. Leo's a funny guy.

MICKY

The funniest. I am privileged to dine on his daily doses of wit.

BART

Well, I thank you for the privilege of getting to work up close and personal with The Oracle. This is a big deal for…//

MICKY

Yikes! You should not, under any circumstances, call Leo… that.

BART

That–*what*?

MICKY

The coy, euphemistic title that dares not speak its name.

BART

He doesn't like being called The Oracle?

MICKY

Leo? He couldn't care less. *Fred Spee* doesn't want that word used. As CEO, he thinks the nickname "The Oracle" is his private property. It's trademarked. Years ago, Leo came up with the idea of telling our glorious leader every day in front of

Gestures toward audience

the brethren, his *divination*—the three things we should all pay attention to that day. The three reveals. So Fred started calling him The Oracle.

BART

Like the ancient Greek Oracle. At Delphi.

MICKY

Yeah, but Fred must've gotten the idea somewhere else because he wouldn't know the Greek gods from the Greek yogurts.

BART

But why can't anyone else call Mr. Sweeney The Oracle?

MICKY

Being the only one allowed to call Leo "The Oracle" is just another reminder to everyone that Fred is in charge. Very insecure. On his third hair transplant. Anyway, when they come in, just call our CEO, Fred, and our Chief Knowledge Officer, Leo.

BART

Got it.

Gestures to papers

Question. How does Leo choose these "three things"

Makes air quotes

I keep hearing about every morning?

MICKY

That's the secret sauce. Unknown even to his faithful servant. I just provide the raw ingredients for this strategic smorgasbord. And they're not three *things*. They're three reveals.

BART

Right, reveals.

Gazes downstage

Boy, you can actually feel the excitement building out there, people waiting to hear Leo's picks. Literally sitting on the edge of their seats.

Another woman, AISLING O'TOOLE, appears stage left, observing them. She moves closer

MICKY

Shakes head and sniffs

Take a good whiff. Not excitement.

Sniffs again

Fear. Each morning, eight a.m. sharp, one hundred senior managers gather here for what Fred calls Leo's "daily divinations." The saps hang on every word Leo utters. Why? They're scared shitless they might run into Fred later in the day and get tested on what Leo said.

BART

Chuckling

Divinations. Oracles. Reveals. Kind of weird, isn't it?

MICKY

Welcome to the corporate culture.

MICKY notices AISLING

Oh, hi.

AISLING smiles

Sorry, but this is a restricted area.

AISLING

Restricted to whom?

MICKY

I mean, you probably shouldn't be here right now.

AISLING

This is where I was told to go. Here. Specifically. Fred, Mr. Spee, your CEO, asked me to report to this area. Even if it is restricted.

MICKY

Really? A new administrative assistant. I didn't know. Sorry.

AISLING

Administrative assistant? The term "secretary" always struck me as preferable.

MICKY

Laughs

Secretary? Kind of politically incorrect these days—says the former administrative assistant.

AISLING

"Secretary" appeals to me. After all, "secretary" comes from the medieval Latin *sēcrētārius*, a title applied to various highly dependable, highly knowledgeable officials. Or even, in some cases, those entrusted with direct commands from God.

BART

Commands from God? Now we're definitely deep into Oracle territory.

MICKY

Stares at AISLING

You're like a walking dictionary.

AISLING

In this case, Oxford English. I try to memorize at least one definition every day. Today's entry was "ultramontane."

She points to the folders

What are those?

MICKY

Papers. Just papers.

BART

Wait. I thought…

MICKY

Okay, fine.

Micky glares at Bart

These are the twelve ideas The Ora–I mean, the Chief Knowledge Officer, uses to select his three reveals. Reveals to which

Gestures to audience

this motley crew devotes their undivided attention. And I mean *undivided.*

AISLING

Ah, yes, the legendary "three reveals."

BART

Hey, how do you already know about Leo and the…//

LEO

Entering stage right

Guten tag. Bonjour. Maidin mhaith.

Shakes BART's hand

That, my friend, is Gaelic. "Good morning" in the language of my ancestors. And you, sir, are Bart Little, correct? Your father is Lonnie Little. My go-to guy in Facilities.

BART

Awed

Dad always talks about you, Mr. Sweeney, and your motto, "*My* job is to make *you* a success!"

LEO

With emphasis on the *you*.

MICKY

And so, the wisdom of the ages flows seamlessly from one generation to the next.

LEO

And my job *is* to make *you* a success. But speaking of real success, how about your mom, Cheryl—my hero, just getting elected to town council? Surprised I know that? Hey, I am The Oracle after all. Boom!

BART

Mr. Sweeney, Mom would be thrilled you noticed her election…//

LEO

Leo, not Mister Sweeney.

Turns to MICKY

Just plain Leo. And how is my trusted *consigliere*, my right-hand… *person,* this fine day? Lavinia good? Over that cold that had you sleeping on the couch for the past week?

MICKY

Embarrassed

We are all good, Leo.

Turns to AISLING

LEO

And to whom do I owe the pleasure?

AISLING

Aisling O'Toole.

Shaking hands

LEO

Aisling. That's Irish. Means "dream." Did you know that?

AISLING

Actually, I did. It's my name.

LEO

Oblivious, looking at the papers on the table, and picking up three, which

MICKY notes and signal by the communication to offstage, never seen, tech people

One, two, and… three!

Smiling at Aisling

Tell me, Aisling, to whom do you report in this *ziggurat* of an organization?

AISLING

Fred.

Beat

Mr. Spee.

He looks at her more attentively

Our CEO?

FRED SPEE enters stage left from behind the screen. He has a determined, fit look affecting a military air. As he bounds up onto the platform, AISLING waves at him. He smiles

FRED

Ready to rip?

BART gingerly nods at FRED

LEO

And *bonjour* to you too, Fred. Yes, we can start. *Andiamo*, guys.

LEO follows him but is surprised that FRED motions to AISLING to join them. She climbs up as MICKY and BART look on, also surprised

FRED

Have you two met? Aisling is joining us for a while to do some high-level consultations. She's a super-forecaster from *the* Harvard Business School.

LEO

The Harvard Business School? Ah, dropping the H-bomb, are we?

Salutes

Well, super! Welcome aboard.

AISLING

It's an honor to be here with you. Everyone at HBS knows about Leo Sweeney and the iconic three reveals technique.

LIGHTS shift to the platform. The screen shows the words 'Morning Presentation' then changes to 'Slide B: Three Reveals'

FRED

Which is what we're going to get to right now.

Gesturing downstage to his senior managers sitting in an open-plan office space

Good morning, everyone. Time for the daily divination. Let's find out from our Oracle the three reveals most deserving of our attention today.

LEO

Shubh Prabhat! Hindi for "Good morning," my colleagues.

A generic slide with the three reveals comes up on screen

Top three for today: One, security concerns on our servers in India. Two, gathering clouds of war with Amazon. And three, you leaders

Points to audience

need to learn the newest methods on best understanding uncertainty. Which, coincidentally, happens to be the topic of my seminar taking place in Meeting Room Alpha immediately after this pep rally.

FRED

I dunno about that third one. Uncertainty? Kind of woo-woo, if you ask me.

To audience

But hey, that's The Oracle.

Back to LEO

He who sees all and knows all.
Okay, now: India. Server security?
Why are we concerned about that?

LEO

It could have something to do with the fact that our workers over there are paid below-average wages.

FRED

I had no idea. So, what's average comp for IT people in India?

LEO

Well…

MICKY flips through the papers, as does BART

AISLING

Quickly

As of this year, $21,325.

MICKY protests silently

With the rupee marked to market.

LEO is not pleased;
MICKY is agape

LEO

That's misleading, because sixty-seven percent of the staff make less than that amount.

AISLING

Yes, but in preliminary analyses conducted at Harvard, we zeroed in on the median value, not just the mean.

MICKY slaps her head; BART stares

Sorry to drop the H-bomb again.

FRED

Kaboom! Thank you, Aisling.

To audience

Aisling O'Toole. New addition.

Emphasizing the term

Super-forecaster! Harvard! You'll be seeing more of her. Lots more. Finance, get me a report on this Indian snafu. And Amazon? Leo, do you have one of your woo-woo historical… whatevers… for us?

LEO

Analogies? For the best way to describe Amazon's behavior, let's go back to World War II and the disastrous German-Soviet nonaggression pact of August 1939.

Pauses to check audience's understanding

Ribbentrop sneaking schnapps into Molotov's cocktail?

Gives up trying to explain

Simply put, we are Mother Russia foolishly trusting Amazon, which is rapidly turning into the Third Reich.

Slightly exasperated

You do know about Hitler, right?

AISLING

Interesting. But wouldn't a more relevant analogy to the situation be the 1802 Treaty of Amiens, where we are replicating Napoleon's strategy, and Amazon is behaving exactly like the British Empire?

LEO

If you want to go that way, how about the 1807 Treaty of Tilsit, where Fred is the Czar, and we're still Holy Mother Russia.

AISLING

Specifically, Alexander I, succeeded by his useless brother Nicholas.

FRED

Laughing

Oh, my stars, I'm seeing czars!

Plays up joke to audience

Pretty good, eh? Seeing *czars*. To tell you the truth, I have no idea what you guys are talking about, but I'm sure our team will run with that… analogy.

Puts arm around AISLING, who is caught off guard by the gesture

Aisling, up at Harvard, you're probably used to people saying, "Let's do it now." But *here* we take it up a notch. We say, "Do it yesterday!" That's how fast we want to follow up on what The Oracle says.

To audience encouraging them

So, what are we waiting for?

Cups ear and shouts as others onstage join him

Do it yesterday!

Regular voice

Over and out.

LIGHTS shift to indicate the platform post-presentation

AISLING

Shaking first FRED's, then LEO's hand

This was very interesting, Leo and Fred. I look forward to discussing it further. I see some exciting opportunities for collaboration here.

Exits the platform, moving toward MICKY and BART to socialize

LIGHTS dim in the break room

LEO

Fred, what gives?

FRED

What? Yeah, yeah. Aisling's a pistol, isn't she? Met her when I gave that speech at Harvard you set up. I was very impressed. Turns out she's a super forecaster. You know what that is?

LEO

Let me take a wild guess. A very good forecaster?

FRED

Chuckling

I know, I know, I never heard the term before, either. But the way Aisling described her job, let me tell you, it made it sound like a game changer. Plus, she's a younger person, and, you know, she's got that whole diverse thing going on.

LEO

Exactly what is *Aisling* going to do here? In her diverse way?

FRED

Super forecasting.

LEO

No matter how many times you say it, Fred, the meaning of the term "super forecaster" doesn't get any clearer to me.

FRED

Stiffening

It means I hired her, Leo.

LEO

You what?

FRED

I hired her.

LEO

To be another Oracle?

FRED

Sort of.

LEO

Like a trainee Oracle?

FRED

She's from Harvard, Leo. She can't be a trainee anything.

LEO

Having two Oracles… is like having two suns in the same sky. To quote the *Měnggǔ Mìshǐ*, or 'Mongol Secret History'.

FRED

Forget the *Měnggŭ Mìshǐ.* No, having two CEOs would be like having two suns in the same sky. Because the sun is the center of the universe, right? Whereas two Oracles is more like… having two hands. I think Aisling will be very handy.

Laughs, but LEO does not

She can help us connect the dots, right?

LEO

Oracles don't connect dots. First-graders do. Being The Oracle means having the ability to see what no one else is seeing and quickly distill that into three reveals every morning. Three shots of intoxicating divination to reduce uncertainty.

FRED

Okay, but isn't your motto, "My job is to make you a success?"

LEO

It is, Fred.

FRED

So, work your magic. Make Aisling a success.

LEO

But you just sprung this on me. You took me by surprise. You, the person who's always telling me, "No surprises."

FRED

Agitated

Surprise! I changed my mind. So, feel free to surprise me by getting seven out of ten successful product launches from your marvelous nuggets of wisdom. Up from your current batting average of five out of ten.

LEO

Who out there has a better batting average than that, Fred?

FRED

At Harvard, Aisling asked, "Why not get ten out of ten, Mr. Spee?" Or even eleven?" Super forecasting does that.

Arm around LEO

Hey, you're still my Oracle—
Aisling's just a kind of copilot.
You shouldn't view her as a threat.
Now, I gotta go. Need to grill Sales
about Amazon. And don't you
have to go lecture people about
uncertainty?

Waves his hands

Woo-woo!

LIGHTS down on platform

Scene 2

LIGHTS shift to breakroom.

LIGHTS rise to where we left AISLING, MICKY, and BART stage right.

AISLING

Can I have a sit-down with Leo now?

MICKY

Sorry. He's giving a seminar on the future of uncertainty.

AISLING

Now there's a growth industry.

BART

His seminars are amazing. Standing-room-only.

AISLING

What specific aspect of uncertainty is he covering?

BART

You mean, there are different kinds?

AISLING

Yes, Leo writes about that in his 1998 book, *Knowing the Unknowable.* In it, he talks about Knightian uncertainty, which encompasses indeterminacy, incompleteness, ignorance, incommensurability, and even ambiguity.

MICKY

Ignorance is my favorite.

AISLING

Might I grab Leo for a few minutes after the session?

MICKY

In your dreams! You have to get on his Outlook calendar. We all need an appointment to see Leo or Fred, or anyone else, for that matter.

AISLING

How about a walk-and-talk after his seminar?

MICKY

Actually, no. Endless meetings. Back-to-back-to-back. To back.

BART

Everybody wants to talk to The Oracle… uh… Chief Knowledge Officer.

MICKY

Not everybody. Finance would rather eat glass.

AISLING

No wiggle room in his schedule? No cancellations?

MICKY

He calendars a few blocks of time each week for structured spontaneity. But even I don't know what Leo does then.

AISLING

So never an unplanned encounter where he just sits down and chats with someone?

BART is about to speak, but MICKY cuts in

MICKY

Never. Around here, our Outlook calendars rule us all.

BART

That's what they'll tell you in orientation. If it's not in Outlook, it doesn't exist.

AISLING

Fine. Consider me oriented.

Starts to exit stage left

BART

The seminar is this way.

AISLING

Taps smartphone

Sorry. Not in my Outlook calendar.

Blackout

Scene 3

A week later

LIGHTS shine on platform post-presentation.

The projection on screen reads: 'Slide C: Do it yesterday already!'

LEO in a different jacket animatedly addresses FRED stage left.

LEO

Yes, Fred. I accept that. But why does Aisling insist on having her own team?

FRED

Something to do with the numbers. Maybe her folks can "out-number" yours.

Laughs

Get it? Out-number?

LEO

What numbers? Is the H-Bombshell annoyed because around here, two plus two doesn't equal five, like at Harvard? Micky can run rings around her nerds.

FRED

Good. Let Micky supervise the new team too. It will be The Oracle slash super forecaster talent pool. Problem solved. Do it now. Or yesterday. Whichever is more convenient.

LEO

Calmer

Right. And how do we get two Oracles to agree on the three reveals everyone needs to pay attention to every morning?

FRED

Leo, have I ever asked you how you do what you do?

LEO

No. And your trust in me is much appreciated.

FRED

Trust has nothing to do with it. I don't ask because I don't want to know how the sausage is made. I just want the goddamn sausage. The really good sausage. Like a nice Bratwurst. A little red cabbage on the side. Served by the Saint Pauli Girl.

Laughs

LEO

Understood. But now you brought somebody in who thinks that the sausage making can be done exclusively through forecasting in a super-rational way about rational people and rational markets and rational everything. And that is just not the way people work—or how sausages are made.

FRED

You're saying you're not rational? That *I'm* not rational?

LEO

We think that we're rational, that if we set our minds to it, we can know everything. But, no, most of the time, people are not rational.

FRED

See? This is why I don't want to know how the sausage is made, Leo. Because you're scaring the shit out of me by telling me that you're not rational. Making sausage is the most rational activity known to man. There are no irrational sausage makers. None.

Sighs

Look, work this out with Aisling, okay? Do it yesterday. And do it rationally.

FRED exits stage left, but LEO heads to the alcove, where, for a fleeting moment, we see his nook with the enormous dartboard. He picks up the darts and starts to throw. Really hard

Blackout

Scene 4

A few days later

LIGHTS shine on the break room.

The screen shows FRED's smiling image with a slogan reading: 'Slide D: Do It Yesterday; Now Is Too Late.'

A single light shines over the platform where MICKY and BART stand.

MICKY

To BART

But what did she say? Exactly? This is important, Bart.

BART

Ticking off topics

Turns out her mom is in local politics, just like mine. Back in Evanston, Illinois—that's where Aisling grew up. She asked what your wife did for a…//

MICKY

No, no. The part about the papers we prepare for, Fred.

BART

Aisling said that from now on, could we please show all of Leo's papers to her *before* they become the daily divination with Fred.

MICKY

Show Aisling all of Leo's papers in advance? Who died and left her in charge? And Bart, please use the official name for our morning sessions. It's "the three reveals," not "the daily divinations." I've mentioned this before.

BART

It's just that when you and Leo were talking…//

MICKY

When Leo and Micky are talking, you hear things we say, but you have to act as if you never heard them. Leo is Plato. Micky is Aristotle. You're Bart.

BART

Frustrated

Micky, you do realize how confusing it is to try to remember what I'm allowed to say and who I'm allowed to say it to? Don't you think we're wasting a lot of time trying to hide things from each other?

MICKY

Yikes! Wasting time? Seriously? The whole purpose of a corporation is to first waste time and then figure out a way to camouflage it. You're adorable, Bart. And, as you now know, I mean that in a *very* non-sexual way. But wasting time? A deep commitment to wasting time should be in every corporation's mission statement.

BART

Okay, but…//

MICKY

You show Aisling the papers *after* they go to Fred. Not before.

BART

She's not going to like that. I mean, I know how you always say that Leo is the 800-pound gorilla in the room….

MICKY

But now there's a new gorilla on the premises. A cunning gorilla. A devious gorilla. A gorilla with *multiple* degrees from Harvard. So, until further notice, we let Leo thrash it out with Aisling. Meanwhile, we hide in the undergrowth with everyone else that didn't go to Harvard and just watch. Got it?

BART

I guess. Who knew hiding was a core competency?

Blackout

Scene 5

LIGHTS shine on the platform, post-morning presentation. Text on the screen reads: 'Slide E: Three Reveals for May 21' A few days later, LEO, AISLING, in different clothes and FRED address their audience from the platform.

FRED

Pointing to AISLING

Aisling thinks that Leo underestimates what's about to happen in our turbulent Middle Eastern markets.

Playing to audience

Under-estimates! Uh-oh! Oracle fight!

AISLING

No, not a fight, Fred. Just that my model predicts a disruption…//

LEO

"Those who have knowledge don't predict. Those who predict don't have knowledge."

Bows to audience

FRED

Peter Drucker, right?

LEO

Lao Tzu. Or Lao-Tze. Fifth Century B.C.E. Philosopher. Chinese.

FRED

Laughs

Very intimidating to have a guy around who knows everything. And now *a gal* who also knows everything.

LEO

I'm not young enough to know everything.

AISLING

Someone else said that first.

LEO

Someone else said everything first.

AISLING

No, literally, that's a line from a book.

LEO

The Admirable Crichton by J.M. Barrie. And it's a *play*. The guy who wrote *Peter Pan*?

AISLING

You're sure it's not Santayana?

LEO

Please.

AISLING

It sounds like something Santayana would say.

LEO

Everything sounds like something Santayana would say. But he didn't say it.

AISLING

He said everything else.

LEO

That one I'll give you.

FRED

Look, guys, how about we get back to the Middle East?

LEO

Said no one ever.

Blackout

Scene 6

A few days later, late afternoon

LIGHTS shine on the break room.

Bart has rolled the cart on during the blackout, and now along with Micky, unloads beer cans onto the table downstage right.

BART

Beer *and* tea? What's up with that?

MICKY

Beer *or* tea. Today, it's beer for the interns.

BART

Beer? What does beer have to do with knowledge generation?

MICKY

People keep the best knowledge locked up in their heads. Give them tea, and they rattle off ideas. Suggestions. Proposals. So, sometimes we do tea. But pour them beer at the end of the day, and you'll hear everything that ticks them off. All the things that didn't work. All the things they hate. Their "unsuccessful encounters with predictability," is what Leo calls them. And those with the liveliest imaginations get invited back for wine—because that's what Leo's really interested in. Talky imaginations. The unvarnished thoughts of the slightly hammered.

BART

You sound like Leo now. You could be The Oracle, Micky. I read this book about how the oracles of Greece were women chosen by the gods, and they gave…//

MICKY

No, thanks! Being The Oracle here means being chosen by Fred. It's like being Captain of Vladimir Putin's yacht. Prestigious, but not much future in it.

Blackout

Scene 7

A few days later, morning

LIGHTS shine on the platform, post-presentation.

The screen reads: 'Slide F: Did It Yesterday'

FRED, AISLING, and LEO are on the platform.

FRED

Snapping his fingers

Darn! I have something for you, Aisling. And you're gonna love it!

Exits

LEO

Should have forecast you'd put a spring in Fred's step.

AISLING

Maybe it's just my super-accurate probability estimates.

LEO

Of course. Nothing turns Fred on more than a shapely, log-odds, extremizing-aggregation algorithm.

AISLING

Was making wisecracks part of your job description when you came here? Oracle *and* Court Jester?

LEO

Of course, We can share that job too. Want to borrow my old Marx Brothers movies to get up to speed? Or Monty Python?

AISLING

Unnecessary. Aced Harvard's workplace sarcasm course.

FRED returns holding a Harvard T-shirt that reads: "Don't make me drop the H-bomb, Yalie."

FRED

Great, right? Fits you to a tee.

Laughs

Get it? Tee?

AISLING

Oh! To a tee. Good one, boss.

Smiling while holding the T-shirt up against herself

Love it.

Blackout

Scene 8

Late afternoon

LIGHTS shine downstage left to a corridor.

MICKY is far stage left on the phone.

MICKY

What can I say, lover? Every month is the 'Mythical Man Month' in this lunatic asylum.

Beat

No, it's just a phrase that they use in business, Lavinia.

Beat

Sorry for my *jargon*, but I am in business, a business where my boss and his nemesis, in order to facilitate their unending, ever-escalating know-it-all contest, keep throwing more people at our projects, which only slows everyone down. And that's what Mythical Man Month means, love. And it also means that I am now supervising double the number of people involved in the production of the daily "three reveals to which to pay attention" presentation.

Pause

Yikes, honey, *you* asked me why I would be late.

Pause

I'm trying to both explain *and* say that I'm sorry to leave you holding the bag. I mean, the baby. Yes, *our* baby.

Beat

Lavinia! Lavinia? Really?

Pockets phone

Shit.

Blackout

Scene 9

Morning

LIGHTS shine on platform.

Writing on screen reads: 'Slide G: Your three reveals!'

LEO, AISLING, and FRED stand on the platform flanking the slide

LEO

Thank you, Fred. And, *Gut morgen, Aun di resht fun di velt.*

To a surprised Fred

Just a *bisl* of Yiddish to spice things up.

FRED

Very impressive. And your first reveal?

LEO

It's not a slam-dunk, but we need to pay close attention to a particular market that I think…//

AISLING

Interrupting forcefully and clicking to show a striking, colorful slide

Writing on the screen changes to: 'Slide H: Renewable energy'

Energy. *Es tut mir leid, mein herr,* but renewable-energy markets are where we need to be. *Macht schnell.*

LEO

Renewable energy? No, we were going to…//

FRED

Rubbing his hands

Aha! Looks like we have another Oracle smackdown.

AISLING

To LEO

Sorry. Unscheduled spontaneity. An analogy hit me in the middle of the night: Renewable energy is the modern equivalent of Iron bringing an end to the Bronze Age.

LEO

The Iron Age and the Bronze Age overlapped.

AISLING

Fine, then when the Mongols gave way to the Moghuls.

LEO

The Mongols did not give way to the Moghuls. It was just a name change. The Mongols figured it was better PR not to be associated with Genghis Khan. So, they rebranded themselves. Harvard Business School peeps must understand rebranding.

FRED

Mongols, Moguls. As the old saying goes: “Those that Khan, do.” Get it? Genghis *Khan*?

No one laughs

Anyway, what’s your problem with renewable energy?

LEO

Uncertainty! Aisling’s theoretical model fails to factor…//

FRED

Please shoot me. Leo! Always with the goddamn uncertainty.

AISLING

Yes, always. And yet, don't Leo's beliefs fit the dictionary definition of *certainty?* Determined? Fixed? Settled? Not variable or fluctuating?

FRED

Ouch! She nailed you that time, Big Guy.

To audience

Not that I'm keeping score. Back to your idea, Aisling. Renewable energy? Sounds like a gas!

Laughs at his own joke

Get it? Gas?

Blackout

Scene 10

Daytime

LIGHTS shift to break room.

BART and MICKY are downstage right.

MICKY

Didn't you already go to that seminar of Leo's? Uncertainty is still uncertainty, last time I checked.

BART

This stuff is complex. If you want to know what Leo knows, you can't just listen to it once.

MICKY

Yikes! A disciple who wants to know what Leo knows. Prepare for disappointment, young Bart. The man's favorite saying is

Air quotes

"I know nothing. Which is more than most people."

BART

Isn't that just kind of a humble brag for a guy like Leo? I mean, he really *does* know everything.

MICKY

No, no, no! After he wrote his mega-bestselling, paradigm-demolishing, *Knowing the Unknowabl*e, he wrote an even bigger sequel: *Knowing Even More About the Unknowabl*e.

BART

Don't get it. A Chief Knowledge Officer writes about knowing the unknowable? Am I missing something?

MICKY

Oh, Bart, the guru is just getting warmed up.

Imitating LEO

Focus on not focusing. Gravity only exists if you believe in gravity. There are no rules. That is the only rule.

BART

No rules? This place is nothing but rules.

MICKY

Bart, the first rule of fight club is that Leo tells you that there are no rules. The second rule is: The first rule only applies to Leo.

BART

Does anyone ever complain that Leo's… kinda out there?

MICKY

Finance does. Marketing, too. And Legal wouldn't mind seeing him out on his ass.

Looks at her phone

Speaking of Leo, my Outlook calendar shows a rendezvous right now with Mr. "I Know Nothing."

MICKY exits stage right; as AISLING enters from behind screen upstage center

AISLING

Bart! Glad I caught you. I wanted to ask you,

Beat

where's a good place to eat in this town? I'm getting tired of takeout.

BART

Good question, but before I answer, how do you know that what I like to eat is what *you* would like to eat?

AISLING

You're smart. Smart people eat at the same places.

BART

Really? You can forecast that?

AISLING

I can. Harvard, remember? Now, how about showing me your favorite restaurant? I'll bet I would enjoy it.

BART

Did you just ask me out, Aisling?

AISLING

Apparently, I did. Now, who could have predicted that?

Blackout

Scene 11

A few days later, daytime.

LIGHTS shine on the corridor.

MICKY is crossing downstage right when FRED, entering downstage left, calls to her.

FRED

Micky! Give me a minute.

They meet

You notice anything different in your boss's behavior lately?

MICKY

Beat

Obviously, Leo is always a little different, isn't he, Fred?

FRED

But not this fucking different. Psycho different. He's starting to remind me of that Kanye guy. Or Elon Musk.

MICKY

I don't know, Fred. To me, Leo is just Leo. And you and Leo go back a long way, right?

FRED

Yes, a long way. And he's always pushed the envelope. But I swear to God, sometimes he pushes the envelope too far, right? And if our envelope tears? Not good. Right? Not for any of us. For example, didn't you and your girlfriend just adopt a kid?

MICKY

Yes, actually, my *wife* and I now have two children.

FRED

Wife! Right! Two kids! Terrible time to have things go south because Leo is ripping the envelope apart. At the end of the day, collaboration is the "Do" of "Do it yesterday."

MICKY

Absolutely. I'll do what I can, Fred. I'll talk to Leo.

FRED

Atta girl!

Pats her on the shoulder

Blackout

Scene 12

Morning

LIGHTS shine on platform.

Writing on screen reads: 'Slide I: DEPLOYING THE ANALYTICAL HIERARCHY PROCESS (AHP)'

AISLING and LEO stand on the platform, studying the slide.

LEO

You knew? You couldn't warn me what Fred wanted *before* my presentation? We look like blundering idiots.

AISLING

We? Now it's "we?" And warn you? Didn't Napoleon once say, "Never interrupt your enemy when he's busy making a mistake."

LEO

Napoleon lost ninety percent of his army in the Russian snow and then got his ass kicked at Waterloo. If you're going to quote military sources, stick to the confirmed winners, like Alexander the Great. Julius Caesar. Rambo.

AISLING

You're so good with history. Ever think about teaching? Maybe start a certificate program in uncertainty studies.

BART,
unnoticed,
sidles in from
stage left with
his notebook
and pen and
begins
scribbling notes

LEO

Is that your forecast for me? With you here as "Heiracle Apparent"? What probability have you assigned to that event?

AISLING

My job is to make *you* a success, Leo. So, one hundred percent.

LEO

Oh. Anticipatory reality, right? Are you envisioning success right now? Well, forget it. Think of us as a disjunctive syllogism. Modus Tollens? Logic is going to make Fred choose one of us. They still teach logic at Harvard, right, dream girl?

AISLING

Funny. You use humor to disguise how you exploit everyone's hindsight bias around here. Chatter on about uncertainty, yet every eight AM work the crowd with your *post hoc ergo propter hoc* act.

LEO

Jealous? Your heuristics gambit might work with Fred but not with me. They don't mesh if you never consider the irrational. Our two methods are apples and ostriches.

AISLING

Consider the irrational? You mean worship it like you and spout defective postulational systems for decades, skipping over essential epistemological questions?

Beat

Until I showed up, no one challenged you on your unwarranted causality approach. Well, now I do. And I'm not going anywhere.

LEO

Okay! The prospect of going toe-to-toe daily with you and your bush-league, jury-rigged telic solutions delights me.

Gesturing

This place reeks of my *weltanschauung*, sister. You just live in it.

BART is madly scribbling away

AISLING

You're a walking Pareto Rule, Leo. Eighty percent of what you accomplished comes from twenty percent of what you know. But you can't figure out which twenty percent. You get snared in informal fallacies and then try to beguile and baffle the ignorant crowd with teleological sleight-of-hand. But you're not for me. Not my type. Type! Did you ever take Myer-Briggs? Because, Jesus, you are the poster boy for ENTJ. And the "J" is for Jerk.

AISLING storms out stage left, sees BART, but keeps on going. LEO exits stage right. BART just stands there while lights dim

Blackout

Scene 13

A few days later, daytime

LIGHTS shine onto the break room.

LIGHTS rise slowly downstage right where MICKY is hurriedly reading a memo in the folder marked with the initials L.S, while BART waits.

MICKY

Perfect.

Hands it to BART

Would you walk it to Legal, please?

BART

Nodding

Oh, one other thing. You know that HR IT director job?

MICKY

The one Aisling just created? Out of thin air?

BART

Yes.

MICKY

And?

BART

Aisling just offered it to me.

MICKY

Director of HR IT? Well! Nice promotion.

Beat

Will you take it?

BART

Unsure. What do you think? People get promoted quick by her.

MICKY

Absolutely. Harvard in a hurry. But in this place, you have to be careful. Changing departments is like changing countries. One day you're in France. The next day, you're in… Latvia.

BART

France? Latvia?

Shakes head

Thanks, that really helps.

MICKY

I aim to please.

BART

Micky, any *new* job would be different. You know that. So, what are you saying? Should I take it or not?

LEO enters from stage right, headed towards the alcove

LEO

Salut, les mecs! Ça va?

BART

Hesitantly as he exits

Tres bon, Leo. Oops. Gotta go.

LIGHTS with greatly altered hues shift to the corridor and to the alcove

LEO

Is our young friend more skittish than usual today?

MICKY

We should talk, Leo.

LEO ushers her into the alcove where he turns on the light

Aisling offered Bart a job. In HR. Well, HR IT.

LEO

Good move on her part.

LEO takes his darts in hand and throws them throughout this scene

Nicely played by the dream girl.

MICKY

Poaching our guy doesn't worry you?

LEO

The job is in HR, the empress dowager of workplace shitholes.

Throws a dart

No skin off my nose.

MICKY

Fred added VP of that shithole to Aisling's titles.

LEO

No surprise there. Ms. Super Forecaster will collect lots of fancy titles before she crashes. Universe Progenitor. Doyenne of Data. Minister of Machiavellianism. Well, Ministress.

MICKY

Not amused

Interesting how people with big titles can be so blasé about them.

LEO

I know Fred. He'll eventually get tired of her. He's like Taylor Swift. He gets tired of everyone.

MICKY

Even you?

Leo throws another dart

LEO

Even me. If he ever finds out about this room, I'm screwed. Shh!

MICKY

I'm glad this is all so amusing to you because for hapless peons like me…//

LEO

You'll be okay. Aisling will make a mistake. Although she does display a certain *fingerspitzengefühl* at times.

MICKY

Beat

Okay, once again, you have to show how smart you are. What does your finger-spitting go-fuck-yourself word mean?

LEO

It's German.

MICKY

Feigns shock, mocking Leo

No! *Mein Gott im Himmel!*

LEO

Kind of means "natural sense of the battlefield." Cunning. The ability to quickly size things up. You have it, too, but in a much less threatening way.

MICKY

You mean "ruthless bitch" isn't how you'd describe me?

LEO

Nobody ever said you were ruthless.

MICKY

If I have *fingerfutzing*, then why didn't Fred make me the co-pilot Oracle? In fact, why didn't you recommend me? Because promoting a gay woman would be too controversial?

LEO

You're gay? Jesus, when did that happen?

Laughs

C'mon, Micky, just keep on keeping on. Soon you'll be gracing the cover of *Gay Prognosticator* magazine.

He continues dart throwing

MICKY

In other words, just keep my head down. Forever. You take a lot for granted, Leo. You cover your workstation with family photos. At mine? A framed picture of a dog. And we don't even own a dog. He's a ringer. My sister's Bichon Frisé. Mister Micawber.

LEO

Really? That sucks. This whole system sucks. The longer I'm here, Mickmeister, the more I think the entire system needs to be burned down. Start over with people like you in charge.

MICKY

Actually, hold off on the arson until my 401 (k) fattens up.

Beat

Meanwhile, you haven't answered my question. Why didn't Fred think of me? Why didn't *you* think of me? I'm serious about this.

LEO

I always think of you.

She snorts

I do. Micky, you could be Head Oracle tomorrow. But beware: if the timing is wrong, you'd end up like Cassandra, telling all the things you *know* they should do and then watching them do the opposite. My job is to make you successful. Not unemployed.

MICKY

Danke schoen.

Leo smiles and throws his last dart, hard

Blackout

Scene 14

Late afternoon

LIGHTS shine on the corridor.

LIGHTS come up on BART downstage right. He is talking on his cell phone.

BART

Dad?

Beat

That's not funny. And no, I did not call what's going on around here a *gang war*. And please do not refer to Aisling as the ninja assassin. When you get to know her, she's a very nice person. No, Aisling is just a friend.

Beat

Stop. Don't go there, Dad. By the way, how do you even know this stuff between Leo and Aisling? And my promotion to HR?

Beat

Leo told you? Why is Leo hanging out in the boiler room?

Beat

Of course, Dad. You are excellent company, but the man is our… Chief Knowledge Officer.

Beat

That's a joke, right, him asking you for advice? Does this mean that you are the real Oracle, Dad?

Beat

Wouldn't surprise me. Nothing ever surprises me around here.

Blackout

Scene 15

A few days later

Screen reads: 'Slide J: Multiply Our Success: 60 Instead of Six New Projects!'

FRED and AISLING on the platform, looking at a very colorful PowerPoint slide on the screen. AISLING has an iPad in her hand.

AISLING

We could make all these things happen, Fred. All of them.

FRED

LEO enters stage left

Leo, you're late. Again.

LEO

Como vai voce, Senhor Spee e Senhorita O'Toole. Portuguese. This wasn't on my Outlook calendar. If it's not in Outlook…

FRED

Yeah, yeah. It doesn't exist. Everything can't always be in fucking Outlook, Leo. Try a little spontaneity. Aisling, your idea?

AISLING

Instead of six projects this quarter, we launch sixty!

LEO

Better yet, 666. My lucky number.

Fred glares

AISLING

At Harvard, there was a case study that talked about releasing a swarm of insurgencies in the marketplace…//

LEO

Yes! A swarm of insurgencies! Let a thousand flowers bloom!

AISLING

As someone once said, "The first task of the strategist is to make resources available and then deploy them."

LEO

Are we fake-quoting Drucker again?

AISLING

Actually, isn't that Tom Peters?

LEO

You sure there isn't a little Warren Buffet mixed in there?

AISLING

Not sure. Knowledge integrates the more you gather, right?

LEO

Yep, you just get a big mixing bowl and throw in your *Art of War*, your Machiavelli, and then add a dash of Tony Robbins, Confucius, and Paul Krugman. Which of the usual suspects am I leaving out? Patton? Archimedes? Chief Joseph of the Nez Percé?

AISLING

Amazingly, you managed to leave out Winston Churchill. And every woman ever.

LEO

Of course, this stew needs a sprinkling of Hildegard von Bingen, a *soupçon* of Sheryl Sandberg, and a nourishing dollop of Oprah.

AISLING

Come on, Leo. What about Greta Thunberg? Get in the ballgame.

FRED

What's wrong with those people?

BART comes up the stairs with a folder for AISLING, who takes it from him with an especially warm smile

Those are some heavy hitters there.

LEO

Mostly not bad. Except Tony Robbins. Complete and utter asshole.

FRED

Tony Robbins was best man at my third wedding, Leo.

AISLING hands BART a folder, and he exits warily

Or did you forget that?

LEO

I guess I did.

Smiling nervously

Oops.

Blackout

Scene 16:

The same day, late afternoon

LIGHTS shine on corridor.

LIGHTS come up on MICKY, and BART downstage left, conferring quietly.

MICKY

Uh-uh, Fred is definitely keeping score.

BART

But Fred always says that he's not keeping score.

MICKY

Who says what they mean all the time, Bart?

BART

How do I function when I never know who's telling the truth? Sometimes I think I'd be better off working with my dad down in the boiler room.

MICKY

And deprive me of my in-the-know assistant? My cat's paw? No way. Anyway, this gig pays better.

BART

Painfully

Yes, but…. Look, Micky, I took the HR IT job with Aisling. Too good to pass up. But I'll still be there for you.

MICKY

See? Nobody sane says what they mean *all* the time.

BART

But isn't that just anticipatory reality? *Ergo propter hoc.*

MICKY just stares at him

BART

It's just, well, I've been reading up on classical logic… Theophrastus. And what it says about disjunctive syllogisms…//

MICKY

Modus tollendo tollens?

He nods, uncertainly

Why? Go on.

BART

It just seems to me that…//

Fumbling with his notebook

MICKY

Moves closer, speaking fast

Unwarranted causality? Or are you asserting that our cranial brain encourages informal fallacies and heuristic hindsight bias? Is that it? Am I in the ballpark?

BART

Well, I guess when you put it that way…

MICKY

Bart, it sounds to me like you've been eavesdropping on the wizards, hoping to learn the magic password, the secret chord, the *Sprachgefühl* of guru talk. Right?

BART

Hesitant

The Sprockfull? Excuse me. The what?

MICKY takes his notebook

MICKY

Exactly. Stick to your knitting, Bart. Don't try imitating The Oracles. That way lies madness.

She exits, leaving him standing all alone

Blackout

Scene 17

Morning

LIGHTS shine on platform pre-presentation.

LIGHTS rise days later on LEO and AISLING by stage left platform stairs.

LEO

Let's take a break on the three reveals today. Tell the *hoi polloi* to go figure out their own three reveals for a change.

AISLING

It's *hoi polloi*, not "the" *hoi polloi*. *Hoi* already means "the."

LEO

The *hoi polloi* don't know that. Anyway….

AISLING

My super forecasts suggest several high probabilities for Fred's attention today. A liquidation, a possible acquisition, and…//

FRED, entering quickly from stage left, bounds past them up the stairs

FRED

Ready? Three reveals. Let's go.

LEO

What if we were to skip the three reveals today, Fred? Let the troops make up their own reveals for a change.

FRED

You been hitting the Jägermeister?

Sniffs the air

Or is this premature dementia? I swear to God, Leo. You better get on… what is it? Oh yeah, *ginkgo biloba.* But right now, give me my three reveals.

They don't move

Let's go. I'm paying two of you; one of you get your ass up here. Whichever is more convenient.

AISLING

We haven't agreed on *our* three reveals this morning.

FRED

Then flip a coin. Arm wrestle. Rock, paper, scissors. Only no running with the scissors. Get it?

Beat

Hey! Three reveals. Now!

AISLING

Actually, I already have my three.

Goes up the stairs. LEO winces

FRED

Beat

Ladies and gentlemen, we have a winner!

LIGHTS grow brighter on the platform—the area around the presentation screen brightens. Fred turns to the audience

Good morning! Another day at the salt mines. Three reveals, Aisling. Let's go.

LIGHTS dim on the platform and rise on the alcove as LEO retreats to that upper stage left spot where he picks up the darts

Blackout

Scene 18

Daytime in the break room

MICKY and BART again unload beer cans from the cart onto the table downstage right.

MICKY

Bart, now that you're Mr. HR IT Director, you don't have to…//

BART

Don't. Please. Bad luck.

MICKY starts to react, and BART puts up his hand

I don't start officially until tomorrow.

MICKY

Excited?

BART

Sure. I mean, more money. But I wonder: Does it get progressively more intense with each move up?

MICKY

Of course, it does. It's like a video game. Playing that next level is like hitting a wall where you can't find your way over. That's why you get the big bucks.

Pours

If you get them. But with Aisling, you should be fine. Given your… *close friendship*.

BART

Today, she and Fred …. Hey, is it okay to tell you what they said?

MICKY

I'm neutral. Like Switzerland. Only slightly more butch.

BART

Laughing

I'm just not used to being around Fred…//

MICKY

Nobody is. Three ex-wives are proof of that.

BART

Laughs

When Aisling told Fred that she respects Leo, he laughed. In fact, it was more like a sneer.

MICKY

Yikes! Respects him? Uh-oh. The bayonets are definitely fixed now.

BART

But she said she hoped to collaborate with him more.

MICKY

Collaborate? She said, "Collaborate?"

BART

Yes, what's wrong with that?

MICKY

Well, it didn't work out very well for the French,

Realizes that the allusion goes right over his head

But that was before your time.

BART

Could you talk like a normal human being, please? Like someone from *this* planet?

MICKY

Shrugs

Saying you want to *collaborate* with someone around here is like giving them *il Baccio della mort*e. The kiss of death.

BART

Aisling was being nice, Micky.

MICKY

Well, *you* would think that.

Puts her hand to her mouth

Given your *liaison* with her. What, you think no one has noticed your "relationship"? Seriously? But, by all means, continue.

BART

Speaking objectively, she seemed sympathetic to Leo. She really did. She seemed earnest. She talked about how they can make their partnership a win-win for the company.

MICKY

Partnership? Win-win?

Exhales

Death-match territory, Bart. Romulus and Remus? Sonny and Cher? Eminem and anybody?

BART

Why are you always so suspicious of other people?

MICKY

Hang around, kid. You'll find out.

Blackout

Scene 19

A few days later

LIGHTS shine on the platform, pre-presentation.

FRED and AISLING at the platform stairs.

FRED

Looks at watch

I swear to God…. Do you know where he is?

AISLING

No idea. I texted him. Sent him a DM on Yammer. Even tried to get him on Facebook. But he's not on Facebook. To the surprise of everyone.

FRED

Speaking of Facebook, you should friend me.

AISLING

Technically, you should friend me. You're the boss.

FRED

You're right. I will.

Shows her his phone

Done!

Looking down at his phone

This meeting was in my Outlook.

AISLING

So, this meeting *does* exist.

FRED

Yes! If it's in my fucking Outlook; it must fucking exist. Sorry.

AISLING waves off his apology

I know what this is. He's sulking because I yelled at him for telling some new guy not to disagree with me because I can be a bit of a bully. Me? A fucking bully!

AISLING

Preposterous, Fred. Where would anyone get that idea? But… since he's not here… should we just go ahead anyway?

FRED

Without Leo?

Beat, hesitating

Yeah. Sure. Let's start.

He moves to the lip of the platform flashing his big CEO smile

LIGHTS come up for a moment on the platform. The presentation screen brightens. Fred continues to smile at the audience and then...

Blackout

Scene 20

The same day, evening

LIGHTS shine on the alcove.

MICKY and LEO are drinking beer in the alcove; LEO is in shirtsleeves.

LEO

So, we agree that Fred is a sociopath, right?

MICKY

We do. He's a dead-ringer for the sketch in my psych textbook.

LEO

Which makes us what? Ever ask yourself why we come here every day?

MICKY

You come here every day because you make a lot of money. I come here every day because I have two kids and need my job.

LEO

But consider the price we pay. Think about what we voluntarily endure on a daily basis. Eating shit. Endless, pointless meetings. Kowtowing to tyrants. Concealing our true feelings. Eating shit. Holding our tongues in the presence of *pure* stupidity. Fawning. Oh, and did I mention eating shit? You were a psychology major, what's the clinical term for our affliction?

MICKY

Employee.

LEO

But are we crazy? Remember, the definition of insanity is…//

MICKY

Please don't say it. I'm begging you.

LEO

How do you know what I was going to say?

MICKY

Because everyone says it. Everyone says that Einstein's definition of insanity is to keep doing the same thing over and over again and to expect a different result. But that's not the definition of insanity; it's the definition of an unsuccessful diet.

Beat

And Einstein never said it.

Blackout

Scene 21

A few days later, morning

LIGHTS shine on platform.

Writing on the screen reads: "Slide K: Change Is Good"

LIGHTS rise on platform where Fred is alone. Aisling watches from the bottom of stage right stairs, and Leo watches from stage left stairs. BART is upstage, stage right corner of the platform.

FRED

You've all heard that saying, "Change is good." Why do we say that? I learned something visiting the Shanghai office. The Chinese word for change also means "opportunity."

LEO shakes his head

And what do we do with opportunities? We seize them! *Carpal diem!* As they say in Latin!

LEO shakes his head

And when do we seize the opportunity? Yesterday. Or sooner. Whichever was more convenient. So, when Finance came to me with the idea of splitting our company into three divisions—*divide and conquer*—each led by a Chief Success Officer reporting to me, in a nanosecond I said, "Do it yesterday!" In fact, we will call these divisions—DO: operations, IT: manufacturing, and YESTERDAY: of course, the guys in Sales. And gals. The women. Do it yesterday.

To get a chant started, he encourages the crowd

Do it yesterday! Do it yesterday! Do it yesterday!

Signals to stop

Okay. Let's take a little break, and then I will take questions on the reorganization. Got a question? Go ahead and ask. There are no stupid questions. Only stupid answers. First, though, I must hit the little boy's room. And that is not a stalling tactic. Get it? Bathroom? Stall?

Exits laughing stage right as LEO climbs the platform, motioning to AISLING to join him, which she does. LIGHTS change to Post-Presentation. MICKY enters and lurks upper stage left.

LEO

We cannot let him do this.

AISLING

I'm not sure I understand what you're saying.

LEO

Okay. Let me rephrase it. We. Cannot. Let. Him. Do. This.

AISLING

The three new divisions? *We* cannot? *We*? We rebel against our CEO, Fred, in whom the board has vested complete authority…//

FRED enters stage right and listens unnoticed

LEO

Rebelling? This isn't the Peasants Revolt, Harvard.

AISLING

Which revolt is it, then? The Chen Sheng Wu Guang Uprising? Basil the Copper Hand's? The Kakitsu? No, I've got it! The 1916 Easter Sunday Uprising in Dublin. The one with Liam Neeson.

LEO

Any of those that actually worked is fine with me because we need to figure out how to tell this deluded, demented, intellectually underequipped, sociopathic narcissist that he's finally lost the plot.

FRED

Bounding up the stairs

Congratulations, asshole. You just did!

LEO

Surprised

Fred, didn't realize you were here already.

FRED

Oh, at long last, something my Oracle didn't know?

LEO

I'm sorry if that little aside offended you, but…//

FRED

Why don't you just stop at, "I'm sorry?"' Well, you finally convinced me, Leo.

Congratulations. Two Oracles *are* a bad idea.

Blackout

End of Act I

Act II

Scene 22

A few days later, evening

LIGHTS shine onto the break room.

LIGHTS rise stage right. LEO sits at the table with some empty bottles of wine and opens another one. MICKY stands stage right of him and watches.

LEO

You throw a great retirement party, Micky. I hope you don't get much more practice. Look at all these swell gifts.

Holds up a bottle

From Bart's dad, Lonnie. How thoughtful.

MICKY

You're opening another bottle?

LEO

Why not? Let's do a tasting. *Una degustazione de vini.* Cato the Elder in *De Agri Cultura* wrote that the vineyard was the…//

MICKY

A little too early in the evening for Cato the Elder. Or the Younger. Just pour me a glass.

He does so

I can't believe Fred is letting you go. All your knowledge walking out the door. It's stupid!

LEO

"Knowledge is information that changes something or somebody." And that really is Drucker.

Clink glasses

I ain't changing anything or anybody. And I'm certainly not changing Fred's mind. It's voluntary involuntary retirement for me.

MICKY

Did you even try to get Fred to reconsider?

LEO

I tried. After my *asshole* shenanigan, I really did. Apologized. Groveled. Full prostration. Offered to lick his shoes. Or his feet. Whichever was more convenient. He wasn't interested. My sentence is final, Mickola. The Oracle is banished from this land.

MICKY

Banished to where? Retire to do what? Your children aren't going to like this. And God help your poor wife.

LEO

Well, he certainly hasn't helped her so far.

Brightening

But hey, this is supposed to be a party, not a wake.

Sits down

MICKY

Laughing

I thought for the Irish, they were the same thing.

LEO

Good point. Anyway, I’ve always thought of myself as a disrupter, so now I guess it’s time to go be disruptive somewhere else. I won’t have to endure Fred’s Chinese water torture routine. The thing where he relentlessly asks, “Are you happy, Leo?”

MICKY

You really shouldn't use terms like Chinese water torture anymore, Leo. It's racist.

LEO

But that's a benefit of being ‘*made redundant.’* I don't need to worry about stuff like that anymore. I'm not just grandfathered in. I’m grandfathered *out*. I can say “Mexican standoff.” I can say he *welched* on a bet. I can say: “Did you hear the one about the Polish Olympian who got his gold medal bronzed?”

MICKY

Cut it out, Leo. You want to screw up your severance package? Think about it. They’re going to pay you more to go away than they did to get you to come here. So, don’t blow it.

LEO

Nah, those pussies in Legal would rather pay me than face me in court. Oops, there I go again: Pussies. Another firing offense.

MICKY

I don't get it. Your three reveals *shtick* made this company. For God's sake, you even designed the logo! How can they do this?

LEO

How can they do this? Easy. It's Plato's Seventh Letter yet again.

MICKY

Please, Leo, not your Plato routine.

LEO

But Plato is ever so profound, Mickmeister.

MICKY

Plato didn't work for a corporation.

LEO

Wrong. He had a job as a consultant to the city of Syracuse.

MICKY

Oh, yes, Plato's famous visit to upstate New York.

LEO

Ancient Syracuse. In Sicily. It was its own Kingdom.

Pouring again

Micky, this is important. If I'm no longer here, you need to know this stuff. I still have hopes of you becoming The Oracle.

MICKY

In that highly unlikely event, I won't be telling nutty stories about ancient Greek philosophers. Not to these guys.

LEO

We'll see about that. Anyway, Plato is interested in going to Syracuse because a friend tells him that they need his expertise there. His knowledge. And there's good money in it.

MICKY

Is this made up? You *have* been known to make things up.

LEO

It’s not made up. In Plato’s famous, *perhaps apocryphal*, seventh letter, he describes going to Syracuse. He goes to work for the incredibly fucked-up government there and applies all this knowledge that nobody else has. And do you know what the Syracusan king—the Fred of his time—does?

MICKY

Gives him a generous severance package with an ironclad non-disclosure agreement and season’s tickets to the Yankees?

LEO

No. The King—read, “sociopathic CEO”—sells him into slavery. He sells *Plato* into slavery because he doesn't like hearing what Plato is telling him. Plato, get it? Plato.

MICKY

I get it, I get it. Plato. And your point is?

LEO

My point is, if Plato can get sold into slavery, that should be a warning to everybody else in our organizational knowledge racket.

You ever hear of a guy in Sales being sold into slavery?

MICKY

If only. But seriously, Leo, you'd better lay off the hooch. I don't recall ever reading that Plato ended up as a slave.

LEO

He didn't end up as a slave. He got ransomed by friends, made his way back to Athens, became incredibly successful, and then, according to this famous letter, he even returned to Syracuse, to the same *company,* as it were, and tried to help them *again.*

MICKY

Plato! Always trying to rack up those billable hours.

LEO

But I will take no for an answer. Making a return trip to the outfit that just screwed me isn't in my Outlook. One of the many places where Plato and I part company. Plus, I really like women.

MICKY

I wish you would come back, Leo. Smooth things over with Fred. Give him the old razzle-dazzle. Work your charm.

LEO

No, I've lost the knack of selling myself.

Takes her hand

Your turn, Mickola. You can be The Oracle.

MICKY

I gotta level with you, Leo, the job doesn't appeal to me as much as it once did now that I realize that Oracles can get fired. I mean, weren't ancient Oracles hurled headfirst into active volcanoes when they screwed up their predictions?

LEO

No, that was astrologers who missed an eclipse. Fed alive to famished minotaurs. The thing is, Oracles' divinations were sufficiently vague that it was hard to catch them out in a flagrant error. "If you fight today, a great nation will be destroyed." That sort of thing. You, my friend, will be fine if you…//

MICKY

Pulling her hand away

No, I won't be fine! There's way too much uncertainty in my life. This is a layup for you. You walk away with a boatload of cash. And stock options. And a pension. You'll probably write another book: *Uncertainty—Why It's Never a Sure Thing!* But If I miss a paycheck, my creditors will chase me down like the Terminator. You don't need a job, Leo. I do.

LEO

Micky, listen to me. Please.

MICKY

Listen to you? You? The guy who couldn't save himself?

Mocking

So much for Knowledge is power, "*Ipsa scientia potestas est.*"

Turns away from him toward stage right

LEO

Knowledge is not power. Power is power. Persuasion is power. Selling is power.

AISLING enters quietly from behind screen upper stage right, and unobserved, stands listening

MICKY

Sales? You hate salespeople. We all hate salespeople.

LEO

I'm not talking about sales; I'm talking about *selling*. Getting someone to act, to believe, to be *certain* you are right despite you telling them every day that they swim in an endless ocean of uncertainty. That's *selling*. That's power, I did that. You can do that.

Beat

And trust me, that kind of stuff makes Fred hard.

MICKY

Jumping up, faces LEO

Yikes! NSFW, Leo. *So* not safe for work!

LEO

Waving her away

Fred loves to see someone sweating to persuade him. Sell, sell, sell! But *never*—even as he struts and frets in his petty pace and says for the billionth time something really stupid just to show that he is the boss—never say what you really want to say, what I never did say, what I *should* have said, which is, "Just how big is your dick, anyway, Fred? In meters or inches? Either one will do."

MICKY

Leo!

Laughing, but then sees AISLING

Stop. No, really. Stop!

LEO

The secret to succeeding with Freddy is to *always* remember that his number one concern is the size of his dick. His balls are concerns number two and three. His scrotum he doesn't care about so much.

BART enters in cap and jacket from stage left but drifts downstage, listening undetected

MICKY

Laughing. Physically tries to turn LEO

Leo! Please! Enough.

LEO

The yacht, the Porsche, that beach house the size of the Coliseum. The trophy wife. The second trophy wife. All to make Fred feel that he has an enormous Johnson. Come on, Micky, what do you think the morning divination is about?

MICKY

Waving

Aisling, you're working late.

Beat

Again. Always.

AISLING laughs, and LEO, turning, sees her

AISLING

Nearing

How else to keep up with Leo? Did I miss the party?

LEO

Ah, Aisling, the dream. Pride of the Dublin O'Tooles. Come, drink.

Pours a glass for her

I apologize if any offense was taken…//

BART stays in the shadows

AISLING

I can take a joke, Leo. We have to, right?

LEO

Yes. Hey, now that you're here we should play *Impossible Questions*.

MICKY

Sorry. Time for me to get home. Parental responsibilities.

AISLING

Taking MICKY's arm

But we'll never have this chance again. Ever. Come on. What is this game?

LEO

Something I invented. Each of us gets to ask an impossible question. You take a drink if you come up with the worst answer.

AISLING

I love it! You go first.

LEO

How was *Great Expectations* supposed to end? Before Dickens' editors made him change it.

MICKY

Pip rips into Estella for being a total bitch.

AISLING

Pip asks Estella if they can be friends with benefits.

LEO

Micky, start sipping.

Exasperated, MICKY complies

AISLING

My turn? How much cash was involved in Pascal's Wager?

MICKY

Nine-hundred-and-fifty-eight francs. No, check that, eight-hundred-and-fifty-eight.

BART dithers about entering

And it was Swiss francs.

LEO

Trick question. It wasn’t cash, but a barrel of Burgundy.

AISLING

Micky?

Again, MICKY sips

Your turn.

MICKY

What was Sappho's last name?

They groan

Sorry, it's my turn.

LEO

Waving his hand wildly

Lesbos!

MICKY

That was where she came from.

LEO

Papadopoulos.

Micky shakes her head

Alpha? Omega? Yanni?

AISLING

Trick question. Greeks of that era did not have last names, so instead, she would have used a patronymic, a name derived…//

LEO

Raising his glass

OK, OK, dictionary girl. I'm drinking.

Drains his glass before refilling it

My turn. Who wrote Shakespeare's plays?

MICKY

James Patterson. With help from a ghostwriter.

AISLING

Giggling

Where is Amelia Earhart buried?

Standing and raising a toast, they all drink

LEO

See? You're a natural at this game.

AISLING

Try this one: What is the origin of the Tarantella?

MICKY

Throws up her hands

What is the tarantula?

LEO

Tarantella. It's a famous dance.

MICKY

Didn't stay famous for long.

AISLING

Tarantella. From the Italians. "A rapid, whirling South Italian dance popular with the peasantry. It was supposed to be the sovereign remedy for tarantism." You both have to drink.

They both drink

LEO

Tarantism. Right, the dance to cure the spider's bite.

Dances

AISLING

Drinking and dancing

"The Tarantella is a low dance, consisting of turns on the heel, much footing, and snapping of the fingers."

MICKY

Dancing too

Much footing, Much, much footing.

All dance as the lights fade; BART edges away

Blackout

Scene 23

The next morning

LIGHTS shine on corridor and alcove interior.

As the lights shift, BART enters from stage right, speaking on his smartphone. As he speaks, he crosses slowly to the alcove, where the lights come up on LEO, throwing darts.

BART

Yes, sir.

Beat

Yes, *Fred*. It's happening now. I had to find him, but....

Beat

Got it. Will do. Yes, do it now. I mean, yesterday.

Reaching the alcove, he cautiously steps into that space

LEO

Without looking, still throwing darts

Hello, Bart. I predicted it would be you.

Taps his head

Super forecaster of doom.

BART

Very sorry, Leo.

LEO throws a final dart and reacts

I really am.

LEO

Ready to go when you are. Give my best to the warden.

BART

Checks his phone to read a list

I need to collect…//

LEO

Hands BART a bag with "I know nothing" printed on it

Company phone, ID badge. Credit cards. Business cards. Playing cards.

BART

This is terrible.

They walk together toward the stage right exit

LEO

No, being a Jets fan is terrible. Flesh-eating bacteria are terrible. This? It's just awkward. Give my best to your mom, and tell your dad I'm sorry that I didn't…//

AISLING, entering from stage right, meets them

AISLING

Leo. I'm glad I caught you.

LEO

I'm glad you caught me too.

Mock handcuffed gesture

AISLING

No, as the cognizant officer for HR, I had to…//

LEO

Cognizant?

Whistle

Up to the letter 'C' in the dictionary, are we?

AISLING

We couldn't ignore… *comments* that were…//

LEO

You mean talking about Fred's microscopic dick?

BART

Leo!

LEO

They can't fire you twice, son. It's a league rule.

AISLING

You do agree that company policy prohibits…//

LEO

Yes. Company policy requires retribution for extreme and chronic insouciance.

Smiles

Corporate *sharia* law. So, I guess my golden parachute is in shreds.

AISLING

I'm afraid it is. Still, no hard feelings.

Extends her hand

For what it's worth, I learned a lot from you.

LEO

Yeah, that's what Crazy Horse said to Custer. Or maybe it was the other way around.

Waves goodbye

BART and LEO exit; MICKY rushes in, stage left

MICKY

He's gone?

AISLING nods

Why did you go to Fred with what you overheard? That was so unfair.

AISLING

Everything in Leo's disciplinary procedure was by the book.

MICKY

Whose book? Kafka's?

Turns to exit

AISLING

Your emotions are probably overwhelming you right now, so it's okay if you're feeling anger toward me.

MICKY

Well, gee, thanks, Aisling!

AISLING

Please.

Sincere

Look, Micky, employees can't talk about… other employees' private parts. You know that.

MICKY

To be honest, I was totally okay with Leo talking dicks. Mind you, that could be because dicks don't interest me.

AISLING

This isn't subjective. As an officer, that kind of language…//

MICKY

Got it. No dick talk. That goes for balls, too?

AISLING

You're entitled to be upset, Micky, but I do hope we're going to have a productive relationship. We all have our jobs to do.

MICKY

So do it.

BART enters stage right, still holding LEO's bag. MICKY looks and rushes off upstage

BART

Micky!

She does not stop

Damn. I wanted to tell her how sorry I am about losing Leo.

AISLING

We all are, Bart. But this is business. And you and I need to be careful.

BART

Careful about what?

AISLING

Placing her hand on his arm

Bart?

Blackout

Scene 24

A few weeks later, morning

LIGHTS shine on the platform. Writing on screen reads: 'Slide L: Super Forecasting = Super Performance' FRED is on the platform, talking to his audience.

FRED

In full 'preacher' mode

Unbelievable, right? Not sure whether you can trust your own eyes and ears, are you? But it's true. The things our Oracle—Aisling—forecast one month ago? They came true. And what she forecast three months ago? That came true. And what she forecast six months ago? Most of that came true, too. I was talking to our Board Chair, Gunther, and he couldn't believe it. To which I said: Believe it. Super forecaster from Harvard!

Applauds, then holds up his hands

Now the problem is … because you know there always is a problem. If there wasn't a problem, why pay us the big bucks? The *problem* is that even though, as

Oracle, she predicted all these trends, these events, these opportunities, someone has to take advantage of them. Someone has to make things happen, don't they? And if you want to know who that someone is, next time you go to the restroom, take a look in the mirror. Because it's you. Yeah, no getting around it. The Oracle is predicting like crazy, but so far, you guys and gals, gals, I know there are gals out there, aren't turning her divinations, her prophecies, into solid wins. She's giving us the game plan, but you guys are not pushing the ball across the goal line. We are all in this together, but you have to… make shit happen. Pardon my French. And I don't want to embarrass her, but you're letting Aisling down. She's doing her part, but you aren't. Guys, don't let The Oracle down. So what do I want you to do, and when do I want you to do it?

UNSEEN AUDIENCE

Do what The Oracle told us to do, and do it yesterday!

FRED

If not sooner.

Blackout

Scene 25

A few days later, evening

LIGHTS shine on the corridor.

LIGHTS rise on BART and MICKY, standing and chatting downstage left.

BART

But does your wife mind not having a career?

MICKY

Raising kids *is* a career, thank you very much. But does Lavinia mind not having her own workstation in the Fourth Circle of Hell? No. Not when she gets to witness my regular panic attacks.

BART

I get panicky too. I almost throw up in the parking lot every morning.

MICKY

Almost? Keep trying and you'll get there.

Blackout

Scene 26

A few days later, morning

LIGHTS shine on the platform.

Writing on the screen says: 'Slide M: Compensation to Competition to Commitment'

FRED

Stoking up the audience with his clapping

And happy Monday! Are you ready for the three reveals? Great! Put your hands together for The New and Improved Oracle, Aisling O'Toole!

AISLING runs from stage left up the stairs

AISLING

Beaming

Actually, this morning, there's just *one* thing that requires attention, Fred. Not three things. Just one.

FRED

Surprised

One thing? Wow! Downsizing the presentation. Who could have predicted that?

Pointing to her

The Oracle, that's who! Okay, so what's the one thing?

AISLING

Compensation.

FRED

Compensation?

AISLING

Compensation. We created a model from a complex, top-secret set of super-forecasts that my staff got their hands on, and it indicates that a complete overhaul of the way we calculate executive compensation will produce astounding growth.

FRED

That's what your complex, top-secret set of forecasts predicted? Sorry, super forecasts?

AISLING

Yes. We can take initial steps by freezing salaries and foregoing annual bonuses. Temporarily, of course.

Playing to the audience

Then we take the huge slug of money that would have been paid out in yearly bonuses, and slide those dollars over for a big bet on our insurgencies, our sixty new initiatives, so we don't have to wait until next year's budgeting process, where we always end up postponing these kinds of investments. When those calculated gambles pay off, everyone, according to their individual results, will be in line for a much bigger reward.

FRED

That's what the top-secret study says?

AISLING

It is.

FRED

And why does it say that? How does it know that? How can it guarantee that? This top-secret study?

AISLING

That's a very good question, Fred, and the answer starts with the ratchet-like way in which executive compensation is calculated.

FRED

Ratchet-like?

AISLING

Ratchet. A series of angular teeth on the edge of a bar…//

FRED

I know what a ratchet is, Aisling.

AISLING

Good, so you know that ratchets are designed to go up. We hire consultants to see what everybody's total comp should be this year, and they look around until they spy some competitor that's paying a little bit higher. Then we ratchet up our comp to match.

FRED

To keep pay competitive.

AISLING

Ah, but then those companies go to their consultants, who look around and see us paying more, and they ratchet up! We're bidding against ourselves. We're paying more than we have to. I mean, it's not like anybody is going to leave these great jobs at the already generous compensation we all enjoy.

FRED

Becoming agitated

Yeah, yeah. So, *no* bonuses this year?

AISLING

Not this year. But don't worry; it's only temporary.

FRED

Yeah, yeah. And raises? Those are out, too?

AISLING

Yes, and the same with stock options. But just for one year. To build up that war chest. For the insurgencies you approved. The great thing is, the whole initiative could be a prelude to flattening the organization.

FRED

Flattening or fattening?

AISLING

Maybe we should save that idea for another day's presentation.

FRED

Maybe we should.

Turns to audience

So, that's it for today. Everybody back to work. We'll tweak this idea a little. Maybe even find a better idea. From an even more complex, even more top-secret study. We'll keep you posted. For today your attention can go… to your Outlook calendars for *last* Friday's three reveals and just keep paying attention to them.

Beat

As always, do it yesterday.

To AISLING, while exiting hurriedly

Have a nice day.

Blackout

Scene 27

The next day, daytime

LIGHTS shine on the corridor.

MICKY, with a folder, and BART stand stage left.

MICKY

You don't have to do this. We can get someone else to do it.

BART

Who else? She's an IT officer. The head of HR IT handles officers.

MICKY

She *made* you head of HR IT. And you and her are…//

BART

Yes, we are. She gave me this job. And I want to keep my job.

MICKY

Don't we all?

BART

I'll go get her paperwork.

BART exits, AISLING enters stage left

MICKY

Oh. You're here. This meeting is still something you…//

AISLING

If it's in Outlook, the meeting must exist. You wanted to talk about my compensation presentation. I get that, perhaps…//

MICKY

No, I wanted to tell you that…. It's time to move to what's next.

AISLING signals incomprehension

Walk the plank. Go bye-bye.

AISLING

Walk the plank? Say bye-bye?…//

MICKY

You're fired.

Shushes AISLING with a raised finger

Why? Well, "compensation" is one of those terms like "adult entertainment" or "alternative lifestyle" that you don't want to unpack. You might say "compensation," but what people hear is "*money.*" *Their* money. And no one talks about *their* money here. That's for gangsters on Wall Street. This is the Fortune 100. We're too classy to discuss such things.

AISLING

Right. Understood. So, I apologize to Fred and withdraw my…//

MICKY

Nope, sorry, too late for that. You broke the no-surprises rule. Remember? The first thing Fred tells everyone when they start. His only rule is no surprises. And you surprised him. Big time.

AISLING

For the record, the day I started here, I can distinctly remember hearing you and Leo say that there are no rules around here.

MICKY

Reading paper

Except for that one. Sorry if we overlooked that. Now as to your very generous severance package that I…//

AISLING

This is all because of Leo, isn't it? My taking his job?

MICKY

Correlation is not causality. But you did swoop in here faster than a Cruise Missile and demolish all before you. You did become The Oracle. And you did make the catastrophic decision to surprise the CEO and suggest cutting pay and eliminating bonuses in front of his 100 highest-paid people. The top-secret study—was its data from Occupy Wall Street?

AISLING

Data that you reviewed last Monday.

MICKY

Reviewed? More 'glanced at'.

Beat

I eyeballed it.

AISLING

As a fellow female executive, I would've expected that…//

MICKY

Come on, Aisling, girls will be girls. Anyway, some of the morning 100 crew texted your ideas to the Board Chairman, who immediately texted Fred, saying, "Hey, this sounds like a great idea. In fact, maybe you should forego your bonus this year." Fred didn't like that.

AISLING

I'd like to see those texts. Perhaps I was taken out of context.

MICKY

Sorry. I'd let you see the texts, complete with Fred's misspellings and obscenities. But that material is off-limits to *ex-employees*.

AISLING

This isn't fair. Okay, perhaps I did make a mistake. With the compensation idea. Thanks to you. But didn't Leo used to say that the only way you learn is by making mistakes?

MICKY

Your defense is to quote Leo? That's like Bugs Bunny quoting Daffy Duck.

AISLING

You all know that I had a better record as The Oracle than Leo. Who cares about that one mistake?

MICKY

Fred cares. Because now he can't trust you. Going rogue means freaking Fred out. So, he gets rid of you. But as you'll see, the whole diverse Asian woman thing did pump your severance.

AISLING

This is revenge. Pure and simple.

MICKY

More like assisted suicide. Cutting compensation was your idea, not mine. Anyway, Bart will be here soon to see you out. You remember Bart? The kid who worked for me? Your protégé.

Blackout

Scene 28

A few weeks later, late afternoon

LIGHTS shine on the corridor.

BART, downstage right, wearing headphones, playing on a smartphone but also tapping on an iPad.

BART

No, I would love to connect, Aisling.

Pause

But things are kinda crazy around here right now. And you just started that big new job at MIT.

Pause

Next weekend? No, you don't have to fly down from Boston.

Beat

Or take the train.

Pause

Meet in the middle? New London? In Greenwich? Gee, I don't know, Aisling.

Pause

Excuse me? What do you mean "ambiguous?"

Beat

I know what the word means. I read the dictionary too. This is not ambiguity, Aisling. It's just a difficult time for me. Really difficult. Look, let's stay in touch and try to work something out.

Pause

No, I mean what I say. I do. Sorry, gotta run.

Blackout

Scene 29

Morning

LIGHTS shine on the corridor.

FRED and MICKY are walking and talking from stage left to stage right.

FRED

Let's walk and talk. Yes, the Board approved the bonuses. I just got off the phone with Finance. And fortunately, nobody at the meeting asked why Aisling was missing. Could've said she was shanghaied. Get it? An Asian getting Shanghaied?

MICKY

I get it. Nice play on words. Now, what about the press release? Should I just say that Aisling is pursuing other opportunities? Or that she's working out some personal issues?

FRED

Yes. Working out personal issues. She's *working out* being out on her ass. Get it?

MICKY

Yes. And I'll ask HR to get working on it right away.

FRED

Not necessary to *ask* HR. I'm adding HR to your *portfolio*.

Exits stage right as Micky stands alone

You're welcome, Micky.

Blackout

Scene 30

A few days later, daytime

LIGHTS shine onto the corridor.
BART on smartphone downstage left.

BART

Dad, I have a conference call.

Pause

Yes, I'd love to be able to talk to you. Heading down to the boiler room and having lunch with you sounds like fun, but right now, I'm doing three jobs and I'm not sure that I'm doing any of them all that well.

Pause

Leo was more talented than I am. That's how he got to spend so much time down there talking with you.

Pause then whispering

How did you hear that? Please do *not* go around talking about Leo coming back. That could get us all in trouble.

Pause

No, Aisling is *definitely not* coming back.

Beat

I haven't spoken to her. I just know.

Beat

We are both pretty busy. She's all the way up in Boston.

Pause

Yes, I know Mom liked Aisling.

Pause

My priorities are just fine, father.

Pause

Grandchildren! What the…? I'm hanging up now. No, end of conversation. Later, old man.

Blackout

Scene 31

A few days later

LIGHTS shine on the alcove.

MICKY and LEO at table stage right, laughing.

MICKY

That's a joke, right? Do you ever stop joking?

LEO

Not joking. I took a job at Whole Foods in their Artisanal Cheese department. "Our exclusive selection of cheeses is passionately sourced from farmers and producers around the world."

MICKY

Why would the Oracle to End All Oracles take a job like that?

LEO

Mickola, I've always been interested in cheese. And the healthcare plan is good. Their deductible is lower than yours. They cover acupuncture. And aromatherapy.

MICKY

Leo, all jokes aside, there is a reason I asked you to come in…//

LEO

I'll take it.

MICKY

Take what?

LEO

The job. Not one call since I left, and then suddenly, you want to meet me *here*. I didn't have to be a super forecaster to predict that you want me to come back. So, make your offer, and I'll say yes.

She is speechless, and he then intones

Do it yesterday.

MICKY

How did you find out that Aisling…//

LEO

I have my sources deep within the organization.

MICKY

Lonnie! In the boiler room!

Laughs

But wait. You'd actually come back? No hard feelings? Toward Fred?

LEO

The cheese department isn't *that* great.

MICKY

You don't want to talk salary? Title?

LEO

Meaningless. Fred can call me Zoltan the Fortune Teller, and pay me in cryptocurrency. He does the right thing. I do the right thing. I promise not to talk about his dick anymore. Or compensation.

MICKY

Obviously.

Laughing

Fred said he wanted you to be The Oracle again, and he promised there would only be one Oracle at a time.

Beat

But I'll be there to support you, Leo.

LEO

Of course. Your job is to make me successful, Micky.

MICKY

Well, get cracking, Mr. Oracle.

Slides a thick folder to him

LEO

Extends his hand, and they shake

I'm on it.

Blackout

Scene 32

A few days later

Writing on screen reads: 'Slide N: QUESTION TIME

Ask Me Anything'

BART is lecturing from platform with his own slides.

BART

To audience

Your question is, *why* do we even have an Oracle? Officially, we are supposed to call him Chief Knowledge Officer. But nobody does. *Uncertainty* is why we have the Oracle. Firms exist only because of uncertainties. Think about it. The only way anybody makes money is because they know something that other people don't know. They have *reduced* their uncertainty relative to the rest of the world by some fraction that then gives them the edge. The *Oracle* is the person who tells us that *thing* that the others don't yet know. Why not just use computers, artificial intelligence, algorithms for this? All the crap they teach in business school? Because uncertainty is too big and messy for that stuff.

Pause

Don't ask me to define uncertainty or how Leo Sweeney helps us steer through it. That's above my pay grade.

Laughs

But uncertainty is why every morning we come in here and stand at our workstations drinking our free coffee and eating our free protein bars while Leo tells us his three reveals. As The Oracle always says: You cannot know everything, but you should at least try to know something.

Beat

So, let me boil it down. Uncertainty means that you don't know how things are going to go. I didn't know *you* would ask this question, and *you* didn't know how I was going to answer it. I could've said, "Wow! You asked the forbidden question, young man. Please gather your things and leave."

Laughs

Uncertainty is other people. Competitors, customers, suppliers,

Shades his eyes

that young woman to your right, that guy on his phone to your left.

Laughs

It's cool. No one can forecast people perfectly. We all end up surprising each other and surprising ourselves.

Beat

So. Did I answer your question about uncertainty? Are you sure? Get it: Are you *sure* about *uncertainty*?

Laughs and points at the audience

Blackout

Scene 33

Weeks later

LIGHTS shine on alcove interior.

Lights rise on MICKY in the alcove, throwing darts at the dartboard. LEO enters upstage

MICKY

Hi, Leo. I let myself in.

LEO

Günaydın, my fellow janissary. That's Turkish for "Good morning." Annual HR inspection of the boiler room, Micky?

MICKY

Turkish. Janissary. Same old Leo. Anyway, I wanted to talk to you about tomorrow's reveals. Bart showed them to me.

LEO

Oh, Bart did, huh? The no-surprises rule? Three very special divinations for Federico, *El Jefe*.

Consulting some notes

Divination number one: The company makes an aggressive move into the senior growth-hormone business. The market is enormous.

MICKY

The data say that? We couldn't locate that particular set of numbers. And for the

Checking phone

second reveal, hostile takeover of Harvard Business School. And then franchise it?

LEO

Pretty cool, eh? My favorite is the third divination, where I took advantage of some recently acquired inside knowledge: Get into the upscale retail cheese industry in a big way. Hand-sell cheese.

He pauses

That's the trio. Three Musketeers. Three dog night.

MICKY

Clapping lightly

Impressive. Thinking outside the box big time.

LEO

Throw away the box. Blow up the box. Burn down the box!

MICKY

Actually, I don't see *any* supporting data for these three ideas.

LEO

Oh, data! Trying to peek behind the wizard's curtain, huh? All in here.

Taps his head

Just constantly monitoring the opportunity space for our glorious company. Reading blogs, Twitter, econ papers, social science research, your team's intel.

Points outside

Talking to Lonnie down here in the boiler room. Best knowledge comes from the employees. Especially the kids.

MICKY

Bart and I ran real numbers on your ideas. Selling designer cheese door-to-door? That would turn out to be a *Titanic-scale*, money-losing boondoggle.

Toys with the set of darts

Along with your other two ideas.

LEO

Really? Maybe we'll make it up downstream. As they say in the *schmatta* trade, the volume overcomes the loss.

MICKY

Maybe in the *schmatta* trade, but not in this one. Disaster is gushing out of every one of these suggestions.

LEO

Gee, Micky, I'm doing the best I can. Giving it the old college try. Not Harvard, but one-hundred-and-ten percent.

MICKY

Your suggestions contradicted all the data my team provided.

LEO

That darn data! Not the first time I misinterpreted data, is it?

MICKY

But not on purpose, right?

Beat

Leo, I know what you're doing.

LEO

What am I doing? Predicting the identity of the next Oracle?

MICKY gestures as if she is going to throw the darts at him

Congratulations.

Disarms her and holds the darts

MICKY

Me? You slit your own throat just to make me The Oracle? Why?

LEO

Remember when I told you I wasn't like Plato? I'm not going back to work for the schmucks that sold me into slavery. I was never coming back to this job. But there was this unfinished business of making you successful. How to do it? My greatest selling job ever. Three idiotic reveals every day and Fred clapping me on the back and atta-boying me silly. He really would have gone for that middle-aged men's growth hormone. And the cheese. But proving your special suitability for this role, Micky, you beat me to the punch. And if it didn't work, at least I raged against the machine.

MICKY

This isn't about me. This is just to make Fred look stupid. The Board is already giving him the evil eye. By the way, he knows what you're trying to do. I told him.

LEO

And I knew you would, *mi querida amiga, ma chére amie, mein lieber Freund, mera priy mitr*—that last ones Hindi. That's why I had to do this for you.

MICKY

Please! You keep talking about doing this for me. Remind me exactly when my request for your help was sent?

LEO

No request? Well, you got it anyway. Now, Fred has to make you The Oracle. In all honesty, I was hoping for a little more time. How sweet it would have been to see Fred run off to *do it yesterday,* hand-selling designer Limburger and Velveeta.

MICKY

How could you? This is not you, the person I knew, my boss.

LEO

Maybe. But however things work out, you're going to be great. Much better than me. Even better than Aisling. You have a good heart, a quick mind, and *fingerspitzengefühl.*

MICKY

Did you predict I would catch you, Leo?

Starts texting on her cell phone

And that Bart would be here shortly to escort you off the premises? You arrogant, arrogant son-of-a…//

LEO

Honestly, I wasn't sure about that. Nobody caught me for all the years I was making up the other divinations. The good ones.

MICKY

Leo, you didn't make up those reveals. You had me. We had decision support systems. Artificial intelligence. Libraries. Databases…//

LEO

Yes, and every day you gave me a dozen great ideas. But I still had to choose three of them for the Fred show.

MICKY

And you chose the three reveals by…?

LEO

Throws the dart that he has been holding and grins

Like that. Give each potential reveal a random number. Step up to the line. And…

Throws three darts in rapid succession

presto! Three reveals. Sometimes I throw blindfolded. To keep it interesting.

MICKY

Collapses in the chair

Leo, you're insane.

LEO

Moi? Insane? *Au contraire, Madame*. You must not be familiar with the academic literature on this subject, Mick of my heart. Throwing darts is about as accurate as most experts' predictions on the stock market, world events…//

MICKY

I know that, Leo. I read *Slate*.

LEO

Some of my bull's-eyes were really bull's-eyes. The Victoria's Secret acquisition? Dartboard. Cornering of the faux-fish market? Dartboard. As The Oracle, you'll find out that it's easier to sell ideas than to know which ones to sell. Like I told you, knowledge is *not* power. Selling is power. Even if you're selling nonsense.

MICKY

Typical Leo, still joking on your way out the door.

Starts texting again

Well, I don't buy it. No way does some random, irrational way of choosing ideas for a multi-billion dollar…//

LEO

Irrational? Wait until four AM some morning when you have no idea which reveals to choose, when dithering with the divinations is driving you to distraction. When that happens, you'll be glad that dartboard is there.

Hands her the darts

Mickola, you're going to be the best Oracle ever. Isn't that what you wanted?

MICKY

Yes. But I wanted to earn it.

LEO

You did earn it. You nailed Aisling. And now you nailed me.

BART runs in from stage right

BART

Micky.

Beat

Leo.

LEO

I'm sorry, Bart.

Checks phone

I don't see this perp walk anywhere in my Outlook. Maybe the invite went to the junk folder?

BART

If it's not in Outlook, it doesn't exist. Exception to the rule, Leo.

LEO

Laughing

Give your father, Lonnie, my best,

Leaving with BART stage right

And your mom. Still my hero. Cheryl will be our next mayor. My final prediction.

They exit stage right as LEO sings

Adios, Mickola.

Blackout

Scene 34

The same day, daytime

LIGHTS shine onto the corridor.

FRED, stage left, talks on his smartphone as MICKY waits.

FRED

Yes, Gunther. No worries. The transition will be seamless. Yes, I know what I said about the last one, but…

Pause

If you check the succession plan that I gave to the Board last year, Gunther, you will see Micky Cohen was listed as a possible replacement. It's a *diverse* hire. Sort of.

Beat

I will turn this around, and I will do it… yesterday.

Beat

Understood.

Bart enters from stage right

So long.

Hangs up

Fucking ass wipe threatens me with that cute shit? I built this goddamn company from the ground up, I put that little bastard on the Board, and now…

Takes a few deep breaths

We good? Leo's gone? Can't sneak back in?

MICKY

Relax. Elvis has left the building. For good.

FRED

We're not paying Elvis severance again, are we?

Puts his arm around her

Okay, okay. Hey, Oracle! Battlefield promotion. So, do you have your three reveals ready for tomorrow morning at eight AM? Better get on it. Do it yesterday!

Exits

BART

Micky, whatever you need. I'm here for you.

MICKY

Like you were here for Aisling?

BART

My job is to make you successful.

She regards him dubiously but then starts to walk away

Where are you going?

MICKY

Preparing to be The Oracle.

As lights shift, MICKY walks to the alcove, gathers darts, and throws them fiercely. BART follows her to watch from a distance.

LIGHTS fade to black

End Of Play